LIBRARIANS OF THE GALAXY

**For every Earthling (like me) who
dreams of writing books.—L.H.**

**To Andrea Hynes, the greatest librarian
in the entire galaxy.—J.W.**

Text copyright © 2018 by Lisa Harkrader
Illustrations copyright © 2018 by Jessica Warrick
Galaxy Scout Activities illustrations copyright © 2018 by Kane Press, Inc.
Galaxy Scout Activities illustrations by Nadia DiMattia

Library of Congress Cataloging-in-Publication Data

Names: Harkrader, Lisa, author. | Warrick, Jessica, illustrator.
Title: Librarians of the galaxy / by Lisa Harkrader ; illustrated by Jessica Warrick.
Description: New York : Kane Press, 2018. | Series: How to be an earthling ; 11 |
Summary: "When a famous author who writes about evil aliens comes to the
school, Grace is prepared to explain how aliens, like Spork, aren't always bad guys"
—Provided by publisher.
Identifiers: LCCN 2017045166 (print) | LCCN 2017034517 (ebook) | ISBN
9781635920253 (ebook) | ISBN 9781635920246 (pbk) | ISBN 9781635920239
(reinforced library binding)
Subjects: | CYAC: Extraterrestrial beings—Fiction. | Schools—Fiction. | Books and
reading—Fiction. | Authors—Fiction. | Humorous stories.
Classification: LCC PZ7.H22615 (print) | LCC PZ7.H22615 Lib 2018 (ebook) |
DDC [Fic]—dc23
LC record available at https://lccn.loc.gov/2017045166

10 9 8 7 6 5 4 3 2 1

First published in the United States of America in 2018 by Kane Press, Inc.
Printed in China

Book Design: Edward Miller

How to Be an Earthling is a registered trademark of Kane Press, Inc.

Visit us online at **www.kanepress.com**

Like us on Facebook
facebook.com/kanepress

Follow us on Twitter
@KanePress

CONTENTS

LIBRARIANS OF THE GALAXY

by Lisa Harkrader
illustrated by Jessica Warrick

KANE PRESS
New York

Spork

Trixie Lopez

Mrs. Buckle

Jack Donnelly

Grace Hanford

Piper Cho

Adam Novak

Newton Miller

Jo Jo

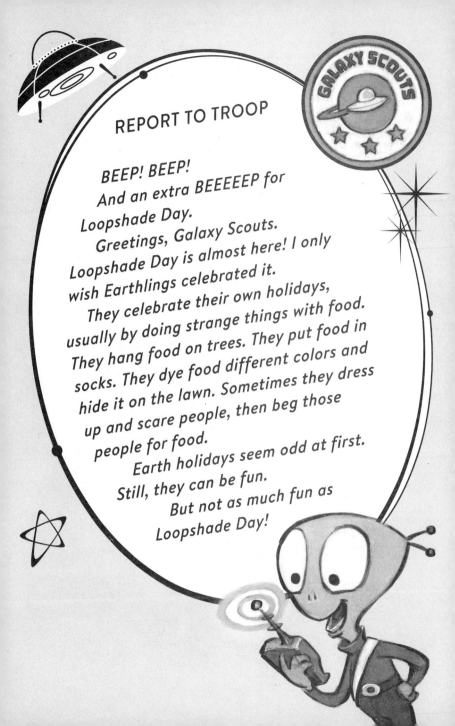

REPORT TO TROOP

BEEP! BEEP!
And an extra BEEEEEP for
Loopshade Day.
Greetings, Galaxy Scouts.
Loopshade Day is almost here! I only
wish Earthlings celebrated it.
They celebrate their own holidays,
usually by doing strange things with food.
They hang food on trees. They put food in
socks. They dye food different colors and
hide it on the lawn. Sometimes they dress
up and scare people, then beg those
people for food.
Earth holidays seem odd at first.
Still, they can be fun.
But not as much fun as
Loopshade Day!

1

READ OUT

Grace settled onto a log. She flicked her flashlight on. She opened the book she'd been saving for this moment.

Grace's school was having a Read Out—an overnight reading campout in the gym. They'd set up tents, lawn chairs, and fake campfires. Thanks to Spork's Blasteroid Simulator, a twinkly star hologram floated overhead. Outside it had started raining. Inside, everyone was warm and snug.

Grace closed her eyes. The patter of raindrops on the roof, a campfire, her friends around her, and a whole night to read—what could be more perfect?

"Look at this!" Jack's voice rang through the gym.

Grace glanced over.

Ever since the new Snooper Troopers series had come out, Jack had read one book after another. He even started a Snooper Troopers fan club. Now Jack and his clubmates sprawled on their sleeping bags, glued to their Snooper Troopers books.

Jack showed his book to Adam. "It

says the next story will change the
Snooper Troopers universe—forever!"

Spork's antennae perked up. He
scooted his sleeping bag toward Jack's.

"Halt!" Jack swung his flashlight
around. "Who goes there?"

"Me." Spork shielded his eyes. "I
brought snacks."

He held up a plate of s'mores. He tried to hand it to Jack. But the flashlight blinded him, and he got tangled in his sleeping bag. Spork tumbled. S'mores flew. Melted marshmallow and chocolate glopped onto Jack's sleeping bag.

"Eww!" said Jack.

"Gross!" said Adam.

Spork rubbed at the marshmallow and chocolate with his sleeve. But he only made Jack's sleeping bag stickier.

"Just stop," said Jack. "We're trying to save the planet. You're not helping."

Spork's antennae drooped. He slid his sleeping bag over to Grace's.

"Don't listen to them," she said. "S'mores are the best part of a campout—besides books."

Spork nodded.
"And s'mores
taste better."

As the class read, Mrs. Buckle pulled up a lawn chair. "I have exciting news."

Spork's eyes grew wide. "It's about Loopshade Day, isn't it? I didn't know you celebrated it here on Earth." He smiled and sighed. "Our planets are so different, but sometimes they're so much alike."

"Loopshade Day?" Jack said. "What the heck is that?"

"Only the most important holiday on my planet," said Spork. "It's the day we celebrate the Great Loopshade Understanding. We make colorful loopshades. They're kind of like Earth umbrellas. We give them to people we want to understand. Every year I get a loopshade from my Galaxy Scout leader."

Jack rolled his eyes. "It's your biggest holiday, and all you get is a crummy umbrella?"

"Loopshade Day sounds lovely, Spork," said Mrs. Buckle. "I wish we did celebrate it. But I was talking about something different—a visit from one of our favorite authors."

An author? Grace nearly dropped her flashlight. She'd dreamed of writing books one day. Now she'd get to meet a real author!

"Next week we're having a special Battle of the Books," said Mrs. Buckle. "We'll break into teams and be quizzed about our visiting author's books. The winning team will eat lunch with the author the day she visits."

Lunch. With an author. Grace could barely breathe.

"Battling books!" Spork whispered. "Maybe I can get my Galaxy Scout Junior Librarian Badge."

"Our author," Mrs. Buckle went on, "is none other than . . . Lucy Harper."

"Lucy Harper?" said Jack. "No way! She writes the Snooper Troopers books." He shone his flashlight over the huge pile of books on his sleeping bag. "That's what *I've* been reading!"

"That's what *everyone's* been reading," said Newton.

Grace swallowed. Everyone but *her*.

2

THE GUINEA-
PIG LIBRARIAN

Grace read as fast as she could while
trying not to step on the backs of
Trixie's shoes. Their class was headed to
the library. Grace needed to finish this
book so she could check out a Snooper
Troopers book.

"Watch out!" Newton grabbed
Grace's arm.

Grace glanced up—

—and nearly tripped over a bucket.

It was still raining, and the roof had started to leak. The janitor had set out buckets to catch the drips.

"Thanks," Grace whispered to Newton.

The class filed into the library.

Jack stopped short. "It's Rollo!"

Standing in the reading circle was a giant guinea pig—or at least, someone dressed like a guinea pig.

"You must be a Snooper Troopers fan," the guinea pig told Jack. He sounded suspiciously like their librarian, Mr. Quigley.

The class settled into the reading circle. The guinea-pig librarian rolled out a cart filled with Snooper Troopers books. "These books," he said, "are—"

"—only the best books ever," Jack said. "See, aliens are trying to take over Earth. But Earthlings don't know it because the aliens are sneaky."

"Earth *pets* have figured it out," said Adam.

"But they can't make their humans understand," said Jack. "So the pets— led by fierce guinea pig Rollo—have to defend Earth themselves."

The guinea pig nodded. "You *are*
fans."

Spork raised his hand. "Maybe
the aliens are just lost. Maybe they
took a wrong turn and crashed their
spaceship—onto, say, a playground.
Maybe it's all a big misunderstanding."

"Nope." Jack shook his head. "They're
bad guys."

Spork slumped. "Bad guys?"

Grace felt a stab in her heart. She couldn't wait to meet a real author. . . . But at the same time, how could she be excited to meet someone whose books made Spork feel so bad?

She turned to Jack. "Aliens aren't bad guys. Look at Spork."

"Yeah," said Jack. "But we *know* Spork. He's not like other aliens. I mean, he kind of is, with stuff like his blertzer, plus how he lives in a spaceship and everything."

"Doing something differently—like living in a spaceship—doesn't mean it's wrong or not as good," Mrs. Buckle said. "Everyone is different in some ways. And everyone is the same in many ways, no matter how different they seem at first. In our school, we accept differences. We try to understand what is important to others. And we don't make fun of those things."

"Acceptance is okay." Jack narrowed his eyes. "But we have to be smart, too. What if we're trying to save the planet?"

Mrs. Buckle smiled. "We're actually

smarter—and stronger—when we accept other people. Have you heard of Navajo code talkers?"

"Yes!" The librarian took off the head of the guinea-pig costume. Just as Grace suspected, it was Mr. Quigley! He pulled a book from a shelf and opened it to an old-time picture of soldiers. "The Navajo are a Native American tribe. They have their own language."

Mrs. Buckle nodded. "A long time ago, Navajo children weren't allowed to speak their language in school. People didn't want them to be different. But during World War II, Navajo men used their language to make an unbreakable code to send top-secret messages. The Navajo language helped end the war and save lives. The Navajo could help because they were different."

Mr. Quigley set out sign-up sheets for Battle of the Books. Jack's club scrambled to form a team. Spork sidled over to them.

Jack held up his hand. "No offense," he told Spork. "We accept you and everything. But if we're trying to sniff out aliens, we can't have aliens on our team."

Spork swallowed. "I'm not an alien. Well, on Earth I guess I am. But back home I'm not. If we were on my planet, *you'd* be the alien."

"No way," said Jack. "I already told you—aliens are bad guys."

Grace set her jaw. She knew what to do. She'd win Battle of the Books. And when her team ate lunch with Lucy Harper, she'd prove to the author—and Jack—that aliens *weren't* bad guys.

3

QWERTS AND YORPS

"In the Snooper Troopers books, what are aliens allergic to?" asked Grace.

"Peanuts?" said Trixie.

"Spelling tests!" said Spork.

Newton scrunched his forehead. "I think it's . . . kitty litter."

"Ding-ding-ding!" said Grace. "A point for Newton."

It was morning recess. Grace, Spork, Trixie, and Newton huddled under a tree by Spork's spaceship, quizzing each other over the Snooper Troopers books. Spork held a huge loopshade. It came in handy with all the rain. Four kids could fit under it without even squeezing together.

Nearby, Jack and his club were guarding the jungle gym from alien invaders.

"Watch out!" cried Trixie.

A kickball flew across the playground. Spork popped open his loopshade. The top bulged out like a giant ice cream scoop. Spork swung the loopshade, scooped up the runaway ball, and flung it back to the kickball field, all in one swoop.

Grace shook her head. Loopshades were *much* more interesting than plain old Earth umbrellas. Spork could do *anything* with his. When recess first started, he had extended the handle to rescue a Frisbee trapped on top of the jungle gym. Then a basketball bounced off the backboard—straight toward a cluster of first graders. Spork sent the loopshade twirling. It floated like a big bubble over the first graders, keeping the ball from bowling them over. Then Spork retrieved the loopshade and

turned it upside down. It flattened out like a surfboard with a handle. Spork leaped onboard and skidded back to the spaceship.

"It's way more fun than an Earth umbrella." Grace ran her hand over the loopshade. It was thick and soft and bouncy.

"On my planet," said Spork, "Qwerts use paraloops for everything."

Trixie frowned. "Paraloops?"

"Sorry," said Spork. "Back home, the Qwerts used to call them paraloops. The Yorps called them rainshades."

"So you call them . . . loopshades?" said Newton.

Spork nodded. "Librarians on my planet tell this story so we never forget.

A long time ago, the Yorps decided to make *rainshade* the official name across the whole planet. The Qwerts were furious. So they started making their paraloops bigger and bigger and stretchier. They became a danger, clinging to everyone, flinging people nearly into outer space. So the Yorps banned paraloops altogether."

Grace frowned. "*Nobody* could have a paraloop?"

"The Qwerts had to pack their paraloops away. It was a terrible time." Spork sighed. "Then the Great Meteor Shower came. Meteorites crashed everywhere. The

Qwerts brought out their paraloops for
protection, but the Yorps didn't have
anything to keep themselves safe. So
the Qwerts shared their paraloops.
When the Meteor Shower finally
ended, Varp Zerpingnut brought the
Yorps and Qwerts together to sign

the Great Loopshade Understanding. The librarians came up with the name *loopshade*. They wanted everyone to feel included, Qwerts and Yorps alike."

Trixie nodded. "So which are you? A Qwert or a Yorp?"

"Both." Spork puffed out his chest. "I'm half Qwert, half Yorp."

"Kind of like a loopshade," Newton said.

Spork blinked. "*Exactly* like a loopshade. I never thought of that."

It began to rain again. Spork's eyes grew wide. He popped his loopshade open and skittered over to Jack's club. He jostled into the middle of the group and held the loopshade up, keeping everyone dry.

"We can't save the planet if we have the sniffles," Spork told them.

Jack rolled his eyes. "Saving the planet takes more than an umbrella."

He pushed the loopshade away. It flattened out, bounced back, and knocked Jack into a mud puddle.

Jack pulled himself, dripping, from the puddle. He glared at the loopshade. "Get that thing away from me."

Spork trudged back, dragging his loopshade.

"Why do you even bother with Jack and his friends?" Grace asked him.

Spork shrugged. "I love Galaxy Scouts. I wanted to join a club here."

"You don't need *their* club," said Trixie. "We'll make our own."

"The We Love Aliens club!" Grace said.

"To show acceptance!" said Trixie. "Like Mrs. Buckle said. And we won't let Jack in. If Jack won't accept Spork"—she crossed her arms over her chest—"we won't accept Jack."

Newton shook his head. "I don't think that's what Mrs. Buckle had in mind."

4

BATTLE OF
THE BOOKS

Grace found her seat. Her palms were
sweaty. Her heart raced.

She'd read all the Snooper Troopers
books—twice. They made her mad the
first time. They made her even madder
the second. No wonder Jack was trying
to snoop out aliens. The books made
aliens seem evil and mean.

Trixie, Newton, and Spork squeezed into chairs beside her. They were Team Loopshade.

The library was crowded with all the other teams in their school—and with the buckets Mr. Quigley had set out to catch the drips. Grace had never known it to rain so long or so hard.

Bzzzt. Mr. Quigley pushed a buzzer on the judges' table. "Welcome to Battle of the Books. Mrs. Buckle will ask the questions. I'll keep score. Good luck, and may the best team win!"

All through the morning, teams faced off. Teams that won moved on. Teams that lost were knocked out of the competition.

Finally, only two teams were left:
Team Loopshade and Jack's team, the
Snoops.

"The final round," said Mrs. Buckle,
"is for the championship."

She turned to Team Loopshade. "Who
is Rollo's assistant?" she asked.

Grace breathed in relief. She knew
this one.

"Roxie," she said. "The raccoon who sneaks in through the dog door."

"Correct!" Mrs. Buckle turned to the Snoops. "Where is the Snooper Troopers' secret headquarters?"

"The doghouse at the pet store," said Jack.

"Correct!" Mrs. Buckle said. "Team Loopshade, what do the Snooper Troopers do with aliens they catch?"

"Take them to the pound," said Newton.

Mrs. Buckle kept asking questions. Grace's team kept answering them correctly . . . but so did Jack's. At the end of the round, both teams were tied.

Trixie studied the scoreboard. "Now what?"

"A tiebreaker round," Mr. Quigley said.

Mrs. Buckle began asking questions.

They finished the tiebreaker.

Then another.

And another.

The questions kept getting harder, but the two teams kept answering.

Mrs. Buckle turned to Team Loopshade. "In Book Three, who lured the aliens from hiding with chocolate cupcakes?"

Grace opened her mouth. Grace's whole team opened their mouths.

Nothing came out.

"They don't know." Jack turned

to Adam, his eyes wide. "They don't
know!"

Grace swallowed. She *didn't* know.
She searched her brain for an answer.
And found . . . nothing.

 The buzzer buzzed.

"Team Loopshade has missed its first
question," said Mr. Quigley.

Mrs. Buckle turned to the Snoops.
"In Book Three—"

"Priscilla." Jack shot Grace a
triumphant smile. "The parrot who lives
in the bakery."

"Correct," said Mrs. Buckle. "We
have our winners!"

"Yes!" Jack pumped his fist in the air.

Adam grabbed him in a bear hug.
The Snoops whooped and hollered.

Grace still had her mouth open. She couldn't believe it. It was her chance to have lunch with an author. It was her chance to tell Lucy Harper that aliens weren't bad guys. It was her chance to stand up for Spork.

And she had lost.

5

THE GREAT LOOPSHADE UNDERSTANDING

Grace clutched the list in her hand. She'd written down all the great things about aliens, and she would find a way to give it to Lucy Harper. She would.

It was the day of the author visit. The whole school had crowded into the gym.

"How exciting!" Spork whispered to Grace. "An author visit and Loopshade

Day, all in the same morning." He'd brought his loopshade to honor the big day.

Mr. Quigley strode onto the stage. "Let me introduce one of our favorite authors," he said. "Lucy Harper."

The gym erupted in cheers.

Lucy Harper took the microphone. As rain pattered on the roof, she talked about books and writing and getting story ideas.

"I'm working on Book Seven," she said. "I want to put a twist in the story, but I'm stuck."

Then she said she had time for a few questions.

This was Grace's chance! She thrust her hand into the air.

Two seats down, Jack also had his hand up. Grace groaned. Jack and his club were already having lunch with Lucy Harper. Did he have to hog the questions, too?

She rolled her eyes—and noticed a damp spot on the ceiling above the stage. It seemed to be growing. But she ignored it and waved her hand at Mr. Quigley.

Mr. Quigley took the microphone to

a first grader to ask a question.

Then a fourth grader.

Grace waved harder. She saw Jack waving, but he had an eye on the growing damp circle, too.

"One more question," said Lucy Harper.

Grace gasped. The circle began to bulge out into a giant, rain-filled plaster bubble—right over Lucy Harper's head!

Mr. Quigley reached Grace's row. He held out the microphone.

Grace and Jack both grabbed it.

"Loopshade!" they shouted.

Spork's antenna quivered. He spotted

the bubble. In one smooth motion, he
popped open his giant loopshade and
flung it toward the stage. The thick, soft
canopy of the loopshade twirled above
Lucy Harper's head.

The plaster bubble burst.

Water gushed from the ceiling and
splattered onto the stage.

Kindergartners shrieked.

But on the stage, under the loopshade, Lucy Harper stayed dry.

When the downpour stopped, Lucy Harper peeked out. Her mouth was a wide O.

She blinked at Grace and Jack. "How did you do that?"

"It wasn't us," said Grace.

"It was Spork," said Jack. "He's . . . well, he's an alien."

Lucy Harper gaped. "An—"

Spork splashed onstage to retrieve his loopshade.

"—alien?" Lucy Harper stared at Spork. "You . . . you . . . you're real!"

"Don't worry," said Jack. "Spork's a regular old alien, not cool and evil like *your* aliens."

Grace jumped to her feet. "Aliens *are* cool!" she said. "But they're not evil."

She shot an angry look at Jack, then turned to Lucy Harper.

"Aliens are friendly. And brave. And smart." Grace began reading from her list. This was her chance. She couldn't forget anything important. "Aliens like to explore and meet new people. But they don't invade other people's planets."

"Unless it's an accident," said Spork.

Lucy Harper seemed to have forgotten how to blink. "Unless it's an accident," she murmured.

"But even then," Grace insisted, "they don't try to take over. They get to know people and accept them."

She looked up from her list. "Aliens

make great friends and excellent third graders," she told Lucy Harper. "I wish you'd put *that* in your books."

Jack's face turned red. He stared at his shoes. "Grace is right. I got so lost in the Snooper Troopers universe that I kind of forgot." He looked up at Spork. "Sorry, buddy. That was a pretty cool move with the loopshade!"

Spork shrugged. "It's okay. A lot happens on Earth. I forget stuff all the time."

Lucy Harper was still staring at Spork. "You're so much different from—from—"

"From the aliens in your books?" said Spork.

Lucy Harper nodded. "You're more

interesting. And more real." She touched Spork's arm. "If I'd known you before, I would've written the aliens differently."

"There's always Book Seven," said Grace.

"Book Seven." Lucy Harper looked up in surprise. A smile spread across her face. "Friendly aliens! That's the twist I need. The aliens aren't bad. They just made a wrong turn and accidentally crashed into Earth." She turned to Spork. "You're an expert on aliens and outer space."

"And accidental crashes," said Spork.

"Would you help me with this book so I get my facts right?" Lucy Harper asked.

"Now that," said Spork, "is something I can accept."

REPORT TO TROOP

Beep! Beep!
Guess what? I'm in a book!
Well, not me exactly. But my name is. Snooper Troopers Book Seven is finally out. The first page is a Note from the Author:

To Spork: Without your special talents and traditions, this book would not be possible. And thanks for the loopshade.

I'm sending some copies to our librarian back at home. She'll probably send them to another librarian.
And another.
And another.
Glarps! One day I could be famous across the galaxy!

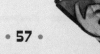

Greetings!
I'm glad we're learning about accepting differences, because being from another planet makes me different from my Earthling friends. Would you accept me if I crash-landed on your playground? Take this quiz and see!
—Spork

(There can be more than one right answer.)

1. You want to start a "We Love Aliens" club, like Grace did. How can your club show acceptance?
   a. Only allow kids in your class to join the club.
   b. Let in anyone who can pass an alien trivia test.
   c. Have a meeting where your classmates can learn about aliens and invite everyone to come.
   d. Only take kids who aren't in any other clubs.

2. The new student in your class speaks another language. What can you do to accept her even though it might be difficult to communicate?
   a. Use hand signals to ask her to play yubble at recess.
   b. Ask your teacher to help you learn a few words in the new student's language.
   c. Tell your friends that once the new student learns English, she can join your club.
   d. Suggest the new student play with a second grader who speaks the same language.

3. Your yubble team captain says she doesn't want kids who are slow runners on her team. What do you do?
   a. Quietly tell her it isn't nice to exclude players.
   b. Remind her that even though some players aren't fast, they might be good at handling vorbets.
   c. Suggest the slow runners play four-square.
   d. Quit the game.

4. Your Battle of the Books team includes three of your friends plus one student you've never met. How can you make him feel like a part of the team?
   a. Study for the Battle during the sleepover you already had planned with your three friends.
   b. Invite the whole team to the library to study.
   c. Introduce yourself to the kid you don't know. Ask him some questions so you can get to know him.
   d. Quiz him about the books to make sure he knows enough to be on your team!

Answers:
1. Excluding people from a club does not show acceptance. So c—having an open meeting for everyone—is the best thing to do.
2. It would be hard for any kid to go to a school where they did not understand the language, so anything you can do to help would probably make her feel accepted. Hand signals are a fun way to communicate when you don't speak the same language, so a is a great answer. B is also a good way to show kindness and acceptance. Suggesting the new student go play with someone who speaks their language might help, but doesn't show acceptance, so d is not the best. C doesn't show acceptance, either.
3. Reminding the captain to be accepting and that everyone has different talents would be great things to do, so the best answers are a and b.
4. Quizzing one person is not accepting, so answer d is not a good choice. Also, you would not want to have a study session without one member of the team, so a is out. Answers b and c are good. They help you get to know your teammate better so you can all be ready for the Battle.

Code Talkers

I couldn't stop thinking about what Mrs. Buckle told the class about the Navajo Code Talkers and how they made up an unbreakable code to transmit top-secret messages. I created a code to use with my friends in the Galaxy Scouts. Can you crack the message I sent?

A	B	C	D	E	F	G
⧗	□	☺	❖	Ω	✓	◆

H	I	J	K	L	M	N
⇉	○	⌐	◉	▤	▽	≋

O	P	Q	R	S	T	U
◗	↺	◆	⌒⌒	✋	◀	❄

V	W	X	Y	Z
⊠	⌂	⌘	⌒	∿

_____   _____   _____

Bonus: Make your own coded messages for your friends. You can use my code or create your own.

Answer: Send more Gloop!

MEET THE AUTHOR AND ILLUSTRATOR

LISA HARKRADER lives and writes in a small town in Kansas. She tries to act like a proper Earthling, but usually feels more like an alien.

JESSICA WARRICK has illustrated lots of picture books about dogs, cats, and kids, but she is mostly interested in drawing aliens, for some strange reason. She does a pretty good job acting like an Earthling . . . most of the time.

Spork just landed on Earth, and look, he already has lots of fans!

★ **Moonbeam Children's Book Awards Gold Medal**
Best Book Series—Chapter Books

★ **Moonbeam Children's Book Awards Silver Medal**
Juvenile Fiction—Early Reader/Chapter Books
for book #1 *Spork Out of Orbit*

"Young readers are going to love this series! Spork is a funny and unexpected main character. Kids will love his antics and sweet disposition. Teachers and parents will appreciate the subtle messages embedded in the stories. The kids in the stories genuinely like each other, which I found refreshing. I will be giving these books to my young friends."—**Ron Roy**, author of A to Z Mysteries, Calendar Mysteries, and Capital Mysteries

"A breezy, humorous lesson in honesty that never stoops to didacticism. The other three volumes publishing simultaneously address similarly weighty lessons—lying, shyness, bullying, and responsibility—all with a multicultural cast of Everykids. . . . A good choice for those new to chapters."
—**Kirkus** for book #1 *Spork Out of Orbit*

"This is a book where readers, kids, and aliens learn together, experiencing how words and choices affect all of us. It's simple, elegant, and very insightful storytelling. *Greetings, Sharkling!* doesn't waste a single page of opportunity."
—**The San Francisco Book Review**

"I'm so glad Spork landed on Earth! His misadventures are playful and sweet, and I love the clever wordplay!"
—**Becca Zerkin**, former children's book reviewer for the *New York Times Book Review* and *School Library Journal*

"Kids will love reading about Spork. Parents, teachers, and librarians will love reading aloud this series to those same kids."—**Rob Reid**, author of *Silly Books to Read Aloud*

How to Be an Earthling
Winner of the Moonbeam Gold Medal
for Best Chapter Book Series!

Respect

Honesty

Responsibility

Courage

Kindness

Perseverance

Citizenship

Self-Control

Patience

Generosity

Acceptance

Cooperation

 To learn more about Spork, go to kanepress.com

Check out Kane Press

Harkrader, Lisa.

Animal Ant Librarians of the galaxy.
Winner of two *Learning* Magazine Teachers' Choice Awards
"A great product for any class learning about letters!"
—*Teachers' Choice Award reviewer comment*

Holidays & Heroes (Grades 1–4 • Ages 6–10)
"Commemorates the influential figures behind important American
celebrations. This volume emphasizes the importance of lofty ambitions
and fortitude in the face of adversity…"—*Booklist* (for *Let's Celebrate Martin
Luther King Jr. Day*)

Let's Read Together® (Grades PreK–3 • Ages 4–8)
"Storylines are silly and inventive, and recall Dr. Seuss's *Cat in the Hat*
for the building of rhythm and rhyming words."—*School Library Journal*

Makers Make It Work™ (Grades K–3 • Ages 5–8)
Fun easy-to-read stories tied into the growing Makers Movement.

Math Matters® (Grades K–3 • Ages 5–8)
Winner of a *Learning* Magazine Teachers' Choice Award
"These cheerfully illustrated titles offer primary-grade
children practice in math as well as reading."—*Booklist*

The Milo & Jazz Mysteries® (Grades 2–5 • Ages 7–11)
"Gets it just right."—*Booklist*, starred review (for *The Case
of the Stinky Socks*); *Book Links'* Best New Books for
the Classroom

Mouse Math® (Grades PreK & up • Ages 4 & up)
"The Mouse Math series is a great way to integrate math and literacy into
your early childhood curriculum. My students thoroughly enjoyed these
books."—*Teaching Children Mathematics*

Science Solves It!® (Grades K–3 • Ages 5–8)
"The Science Solves It! series is a wonderful tool for
the elementary teacher who wants to integrate reading
and science."—*National Science Teachers Association*

Social Studies Connects® (Grades K–3 • Ages 5–8)
"This series is very strongly recommended…."—*Children's Bookwatch*
"Well done!"—*School Library Journal*